424

DATE DUE

APR 5 2	MAN 4	
NOV 15 2	MAY 0 6	
JAN 10 3	JAN 5 12	
JAN 25 3	MAY 5 1987	
FEB 8 2		
FEB 22 2		
APR 10 4		
MAY 10 2		
DEC 18 2		
OCT 24		
OCT 16 2		

GAYLORD 234   PRINTED IN U.S.A.

424

E
S

Scott, Ann Herbert
Not just one

For my Father and Mother

NOT JUST ONE

Ann Herbert Scott

Illustrated by
Yaroslava

Lothrop, Lee & Shepard Co., Inc.
New York

Text copyright © 1968 by Ann Herbert Scott
Illustrations copyright © 1968 by Yaroslava Mills
Library of Congress Catalog Card Number: 68-14072
Manufactured in the United States of America
1 2 3 4 5 72 71 70 69 68

The little girl's mother was baking.
The sweet smell of cookies filled the kitchen.

"Mmmmmmm," said the little girl. "May I have a cookie?"

Her mother nodded. "Yes, you may, love," she said.

Some day I'll make cookies,
the little girl thought to herself.
I'll make brown ones and round ones,
fat puffy ones and tiny crispy ones,
stars and hearts and gingerbread men.
I'll even have a cookie store of my
own. Then all day long I can nibble
on cookies and give lots away
when my friends stop by.

"Please," the little girl asked her mother,
"may I have two cookies?"

"We'll be having lunch soon," her mother said.
"You may have just one."

That afternoon a carnival came
to the little girl's street. "Let's go see,"
cried the little girl, tugging at her mother's hand.

On the first corner they met a man
selling balloons. "Buy your balloons here!"
he shouted. "Big, beautiful balloons!"
Dancing at the ends of the strings in his hand were
more balloons than the little girl had ever seen.

"Please," she begged, "may I have a balloon?"

"Yes." Her mother smiled.

I'll go dancing, too, thought the little girl,
high in the sky with clouds of balloons.
I'll be the queen of all the balloons and wherever
I dance, there will be balloons—
millions and trillions of bouncing balloons.

She jumped up and down with excitement.
"Mama," she said, "I'd like a red balloon and a
pink one and a yellow one and . . ."

"Just a minute," said her mother, shaking her head.
"You'd better pick the one you like best."

At the end of the block a merry-go-round
whirled to a stop. "I just love to ride," said
the little girl, looking hopefully at her mother.
Her mother lifted her onto a prancing horse.

I'll ride and ride, the little girl thought,
taking the horse's reins in her hands.
I'll ride away on my horse to
the place where the sea begins.
And then we'll swim, my horse and I,
until . . .

Suddenly the music was over
and the merry-go-round began to slow down.
"Please, don't stop," the little girl cried.

But her mother took her down
from the saddle. "Sorry, love," she said,
"it's time to go home and fix supper.
Just one ride for today."

The little girl sighed as they started
for home. "Why is it that whenever
there's something I like, it's always just one?"

That night when supper was over,
the little girl went down to the front stoop
to play hopscotch with her friends.
After a while, the street lights came on.
"Time for bed," her mother called from the window.
"Now?"
"Right now," answered her mother,
"it's getting dark."

Slowly the little girl began climbing the steps.
Some day, she thought, I'll live in a castle
with winding stairs, and I'll stay up all night
to watch the stars.

Then she looked up. There at the top
of the steps was her mother, waiting to meet her
with her arms held out.

The little girl ran all the rest of the way
without stopping. When she reached her mother,
she jumped into her arms for a kiss and a hug.

"Mama," asked the little girl, "how many hugs
may I have?"

Her mother held her very close. "Not just one,
love," she said softly.

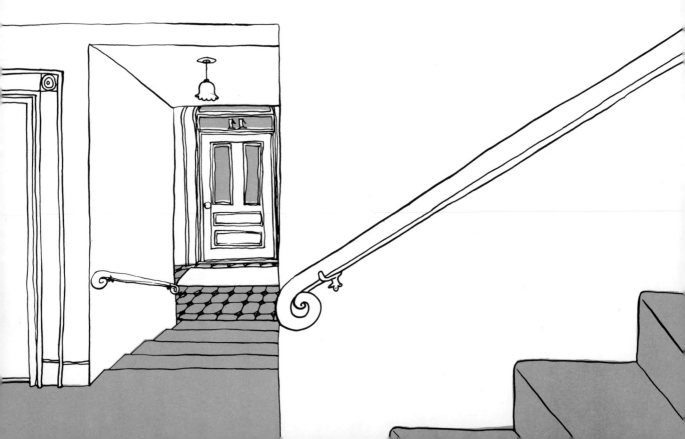

5221